LITTLE
GOES SHOPPING

WRITTEN BY MICHÈLE DUFRESNE
ILLUSTRATED BY MAX STASUYK

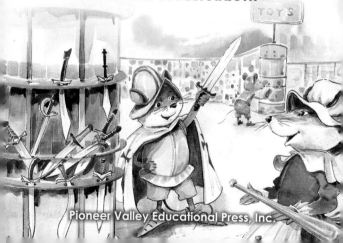

Pioneer Valley Educational Press, Inc.

Look at the helmet.

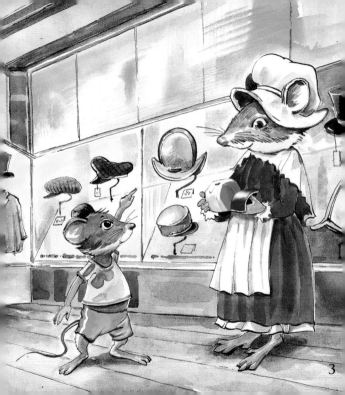

Look at the armor.

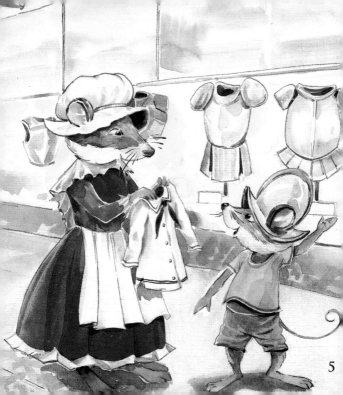

Look at the cape.

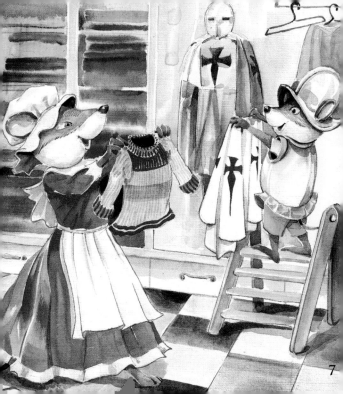

7

Look at the shoes.

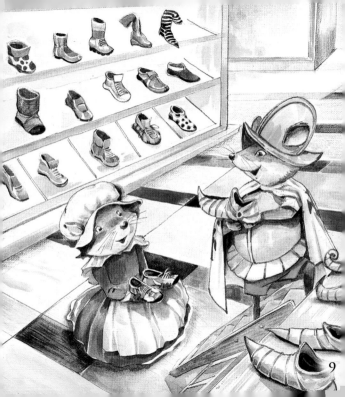

9

Look at the sword.

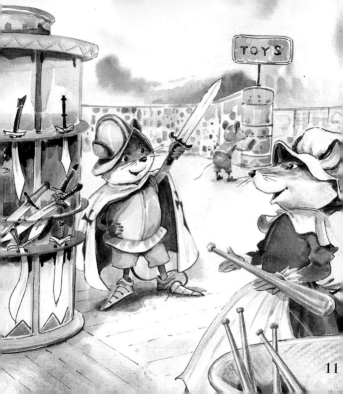

11

Look at me!

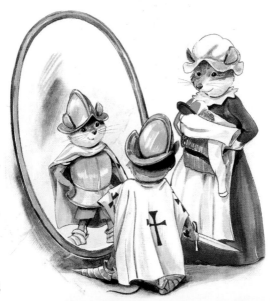